D0245937
Powys
37218 00476140 4

The Dragon Ring

Liz Haigh

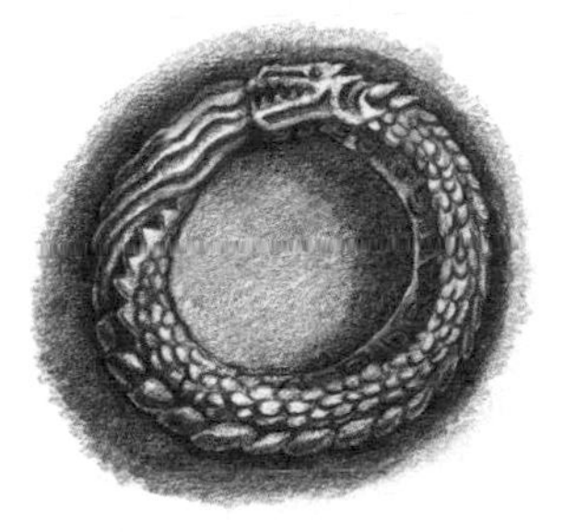

Illustrated by
Rob Davies

First Impression—2000
Second Impression—2002

ISBN 1 85902 724 5

This book is published with the support of the Arts Council of Wales.

Printed in Wales at
Gomer Press, Llandysul, Ceredigion SA44 4QL

To Rhiannon Joan Haigh

Chapter 1

'Look, I've found 5p!' said Louise.

Sara was getting fed up with Louise. She was always lucky with things like that. Louise found pennies behind the book shelves when she cleared them up. Nobody else did. She found any money that had got lost on the way to school. Nobody ever knew exactly where they had lost their money and Louise always said they couldn't prove it was their money that she had found. She had even found a purse on their school trip to the Welsh Folk Museum, but Mrs Hughes had made her hand it in.

Sara said nothing. She watched Louise as they walked down past the school field. 'How do you do it?' she asked.

'How do I do what?' said Louise.

'How do you find everything?'

'I use my eyes,' said Louise.

Sara didn't think this was much of an answer, but she watched Louise even more carefully, just in case. 'But you don't,' she grumbled after a minute or two. 'You aren't looking at the path.' She walked on a few more paces, still watching. 'I know what it is!' she said suddenly. 'Stop, Louise!'

Louise turned round. 'What is it?'

'You always walk in front,' said Sara. 'You see everything before I get a chance. Let me go in front of you.'

'OK,' said Louise, shrugging her shoulders. 'I'm not stopping you. But it won't make any difference, you know.'

Sara hurried in front of her friend. Her eyes scanned the pavement, but she could only see old bits of paper and weeds growing out of the cracks in the path.

Then she saw it.

It was only a little sparkle of metal at the very edge of the path, just where a twisted tree root

came out under the fence at the end of the field. Sara bent down to pull it out of the grass. It was a brownish colour and she thought at first it was only a penny.

She picked it up and brushed the mud off it. It was a ring.

'What's that?' asked Louise, as she caught up with her.

Sara showed her. 'It looks old. It's got all twisty patterns on it.' She turned it round. Spiky lines wound all round it. There seemed to be some writing on the inside of the ring, but it was not very clear.

'Someone's lost that,' said Louise. 'You should take it into school tomorrow. Or to the police.'

Sara pulled back her hand. 'I don't see why I should. You never give in any money you find.' She put the ring in her pocket and started to walk on down the path.

Louise followed her. 'Let me look at it. Please.'

'No. It's mine,' said Sara. She kept walking.

At the bottom of the road Sara always turned left towards her house, while Louise went right and round the next corner. Usually they stood by the turning and talked for ages, but today Sara walked off on her own. She turned round just once, to see if Louise was watching. Louise was still standing at the corner. She made a face at Sara. Sara pretended not to notice.

It was her ring, Sara said to herself. It was nothing to do with Louise,

Sara went straight upstairs when she got home. She switched on the light in the bathroom and peered carefully at the ring. She rubbed gently at the pattern with her thumb.

Suddenly her head felt wobbly. A swirl of grey and green mist seemed to be floating in front of her eyes. It felt almost like the time she had fainted on a hot day in assembly . . .

She shook her head and the mist cleared. The ring lay at her feet on the bath mat. Slowly she bent down to pick it up.

She was about to rub the ring again, but changed her mind. Dad had got out a new toothbrush that morning and the old one would still be in the bin. It would be just right for cleaning off the mud.

The brush made the pattern much easier to see. The twisty lines were the scales of some sort of animal. It seemed to be a dinosaur, or perhaps a dragon, with a spiky head. On the inside of the ring was some writing which Sara could not quite make out. She added a bit of toothpaste to the brush and worked steadily over the metal until it shone.

'Sara, what are you doing in there?'

It was Mum's voice. 'Nothing,' called Sara. 'Just washing my hands.' She rinsed the ring under the tap and hurried into her bedroom. She dropped it into a half empty box of tissues, slid the box under her bed and made her way downstairs.

Whatever the writing was, it would have to wait for now.

Chapter 2

It was late evening and time for bed before Sara had another chance to look at the ring. This did not really matter. She would not need much light to read a few letters, and she had a small pocket torch hidden in a drawer with her T-shirts.

She found the torch, and a spare page in a notebook, and a felt pen. Then she felt under her bed for the tissue box. For an awful moment she thought Mum had thrown it away, but it was still there; it had just got pushed behind a pair of pink trainers that were too small for Sara, though she hadn't got rid of them yet.

She shone the torch on the inside of the ring. This was not going to be easy. The letters were all pushed together, not split up into words.

Whoever made the ring should have had Mrs Hughes for a teacher. She was always telling them to leave gaps between the words when they were writing stories. *And* someone should have told the person not to use capital letters all the time.

Sara sighed. How was she going to find out where to start?

She chose a letter at random and started to copy the message onto the paper.

I G • D E W C H G Y D A R D D R A

Great.

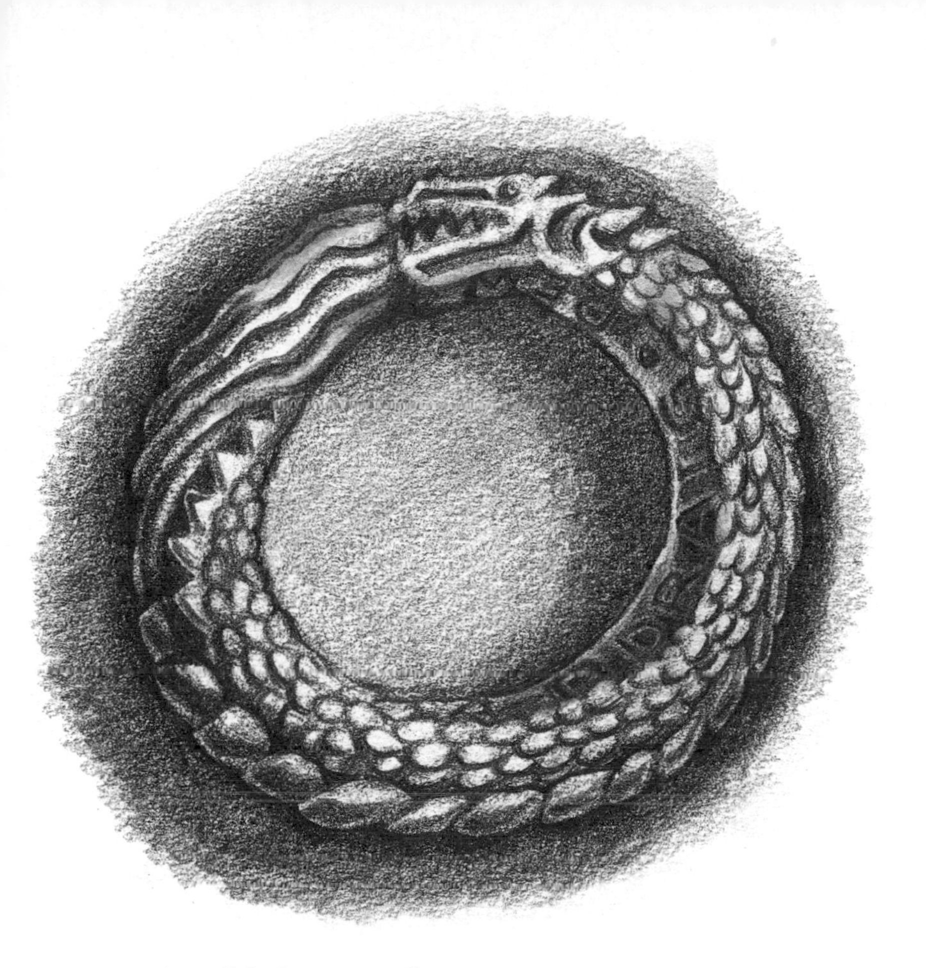

What did *that* mean?

She slipped the ring onto her finger and lay flat on the bed, her head propped up on her elbows, shining the torch onto the message.

Then she had an idea. Full stops! That blob could be a full stop!

She copied the message again under the first one, starting after the blob.

D E W C H G Y D A R D D R A I G .

It still didn't make any sense.

Maybe it was a secret code. But if she didn't know what the code was, how would she ever work it out?

Sara stared at the ring for a minute, hoping an idea would come into her head, but nothing did. She took off the ring and stuffed everything into the tissue box, then switched off the torch and wriggled under her duvet.

Maybe Louise would be able to think what to do. But she was sort of not friends with Louise, after this afternoon.

Sara had a feeling that Louise would somehow take over. Louise was like that. Like when Mrs Williams wanted flower dancers for the Eisteddfod. Sara knew the dance and she taught it to Louise on the way home, then Louise got picked to be a dancer instead. Sara was left singing a Welsh song with the rest of the class and never went on the stage at all.

She started singing the song in her mind. *Dewch nawr i ddawnsio gyda fi . . .*

Suddenly she sat bolt upright in bed. What was that first word again?

The torch back on, Sara pulled a cardboard folder from the end of her book shelves and searched through it. There was the song, with the words translated into English underneath. She grabbed the tissue box and held the crumpled piece of paper beside the Welsh song.

Yes, it was Welsh all right.

Dewch meant *come*. And *gyda* meant . . . was it *dance*? No, that was *dawnsio,* of course. It must mean *with.*

What about the *rddraig*? What sort of word was that? The *r* might be a mistake. Lots of words in Welsh began with *dd*; it made a sort of 'the' noise. But she didn't remember *ddraig*.

Footsteps sounded on the stairs. In a panic, Sara dropped everything into the tissue box once more and shoved it under the bed.

She lay very still, just in case Mum looked in. *Ddraig. Dewch gyda ddraig . . . dewch gyda'r ddraig*. Yes, of course, that was it. But what did *ddraig* mean?

For once in her life, she hoped they would do Welsh in school the next morning.

Chapter 3

'Mrs Hughes, have we got Welsh today?' Sara asked.

Mrs Hughes was counting dinner money into a tin. 'Seventy, eighty, ninety, ninety-five, one pound. No, Sara, PE is on Mondays. You know that.'

'No, not PE. Welsh.'

Mrs Hughes put the tin down. 'Sara, I am trying to count this before assembly, please. No, we haven't got Welsh, except that we'll have to practise the carol later.' She picked up the tin again. 'Why did you want to know?'

Sara said nothing. She could see it was not the time to ask about Welsh words.

Mrs Hughes didn't have a chance to go through the song till the very end of the day. She was not in a good mood by then.

'You aren't Infants any more,' she said impatiently after the first verse. 'Juniors are quite old enough to be able to manage a song in Welsh. Come on.'

The trouble was that it was a song they all knew in English: Silent Night. Sara sang the first line loudly: '*Gyda'r nos, dros y byd . . .*' but after that she suddenly found she was singing 'All is calm, all is bright . . .' and Mrs Hughes stopped playing and glared at the end of the second row.

'One little girl in that line doesn't seem to know the difference between Welsh and English.'

Sara went red. 'Sorry, Miss.'

'Please try to think about what you're singing. It only takes one person to make everyone go wrong.'

Sara sang very quietly after that, just in case, and tried to listen to Rhian. Rhian knew all the Welsh perfectly, but her voice was not very loud and Sara could not really follow her properly.

Nobody else could remember all the words, and when they got to the high bit near the end nobody could reach the notes either. There were some faint squcaks and a lot of giggles.

Mrs Hughes started to get really cross. She closed the lid of the piano and turned round to face them all. 'You don't seem to realise, Class 8, that we can't have any extra time in the hall. The other classes need it for PE. If you can't learn the words in time for our practice, then we'll be the only class not singing a carol this Christmas.'

Everybody stopped giggling and started to look worried.

'We haven't got any more time in here today. You all have the words in your Welsh books. Instead of a story this afternoon, you can sit quietly and learn them.' Mrs Hughes stood up. 'Line up by the door, please.'

They all walked over to the hall door, not daring to chatter. Mrs Hughes was in one of those moods where you could get into lots of trouble without doing anything much. Sara stood very still and examined the photos on the wall display next to her.

The words almost jumped out at her suddenly. Y DDRAIG GOCH. A group of smiling Infants next to a wall display with a big cheerful Welsh dragon.

Goch was the same as *coch*. That meant *red.* And *ddraig* must mean *dragon.* Of course!

'SARA ROBERTS!'

Sara realised that most of the class were halfway along the corridor. Mrs Hughes looked as if she was going to start breathing fire herself, any minute! Sara hurried to join the line and found herself next to Louise. They walked back together silently.

The other children got out the copies of the carol and made their way to their seats, but Mrs Hughes called Sara and Louise over to her desk. 'I want to ask you what's been going on,' she said.

Sara looked at Louise. Louise looked at the floor.

'Sara, Louise told me this afternoon that you've been nasty to her. What happened?'

Sara felt tears welling up in her eyes. This really was not fair. 'Nothing!' she said.

Mrs Hughes sighed. 'Well, I don't know. I didn't see anything. What I do know is that you two have been friends for years, and if you've had some silly argument it must stop now. So will you make friends again?'

'Yes, Mrs Hughes,' they muttered, and escaped back to their seats.

Sara found herself walking home with Louise at the end of the day. She was glad really. She didn't want Louise as an enemy.

'So we're friends now?' asked Louise.

Sara nodded.

'Let's go home and look at your ring, then.'

That was just like Louise. She never gave up. Sara thought quickly. 'I haven't got it now,' she lied. 'My mum made me take it down the police station.'

'You shouldn't have told her about it,' said Louise.

'She would have noticed it,' Sara pointed out.

They walked briskly to the end of the road. It was getting colder now. In one window someone had already put up a set of Christmas lights.

'Do you want to go carol singing?' Louise asked suddenly.

'What, tonight?'

'Why not? We could go out about six. Everyone's in then. Let's ask your mum.'

Sara asked Mum, who was not keen on the idea. 'If I know you two, you won't be back when your tea's ready.'

'We were going out after tea,' explained Louise. 'About six.'

'You are doing no such thing,' said Sara's mother firmly. 'I'm not letting two girls go round strangers' houses on their own in the dark. Off you go, Louise. I don't want your mother worrying.'

Louise realised there was no point in arguing, and left. Sara watched her walk off down the path alone.

All in all, it had not been a good day.

Chapter 4

Sara went straight up to her room after tea. Mum was being really unfair. It couldn't be dangerous to go carol-singing, not when there were two of them. Nobody ever let her do anything. She sat on her bed, swinging her feet, and kicked the tissue box accidentally.

The ring! She felt under her bed for the box and looked inside it anxiously.

The ring was still there, but it was a risky place to leave it. Sara searched in her cupboard for a small jewellery box her aunt had given her last year. It was empty except for a bead necklace and a plastic pearl ring out of a cracker. The dragon ring looked much more valuable.

Sara turned the dragon ring over and over in her hand. *Dewch gyda'r ddraig. Come with the dragon.* It was a funny thing to put on a ring. If it said *The Welsh Dragon* or *A Present from Wales,* that would make sense. But *Come with the dragon* was silly. Come where?

She slipped the ring onto her finger. It fitted her all right. She thought the pearl ring looked nicer, even though it wasn't real. She held up her hand towards the mirror. 'Dewch gyda'r ddraig,' she muttered again to herself.

And then the mist began. It was all green and grey, just like the mist in the bathroom when she had been cleaning the ring the day before. But this time, when Sara rubbed her eyes, the mist only grew thicker.

Sara tried to call out, but she couldn't speak; it was just like a bad dream when you tried to shout and your voice wouldn't work. She couldn't move either. The mist swept silently around her until she could see nothing else at all. She saw it start to get thinner again, turn white, and then, to her relief, clear away completely.

And then she felt even greater panic.

It wasn't her room she was in. It was a room she had never seen before.

It was a very plain-looking room. The walls were painted white, the floor was wooden with a rag rug in the middle, and the bed looked all plain and hard. Sara found she could move again, and hurried over to the window.

The street outside looked ordinary, though a bit old-fashioned, and it was very quiet. The road had no markings on it and Sara couldn't see a single car. It was morning, probably late morning because the sun was quite high, but cold; frost still covered part of the footpath. Sara shivered. She realised, suddenly, that she seemed to be wearing a skirt instead of her Disney leggings. She stared at her clothes in amazement.

It was not a dream. She never had dreams as detailed as this. And anyway she hadn't gone to sleep. She had just been standing by her mirror, playing with the ring . . .

The ring was still on her finger. It looked ordinary, not magical at all. Sara held out her hand. 'Dewch gyda'r ddraig,' she said. Maybe they were magic words.

A wisp of mist floated past again, but it did not thicken as before. Sara was still there in the plain white room, still wearing the old-fashioned clothes.

Where was she? And *when*?

Had the ring taken her back in time?

And however was she going to get home again?

Suddenly she heard footsteps hurrying along outside the room. The door opened.

Chapter 5

'Sara?' called a strange voice.

Sara's heart thumped. She couldn't speak.

A girl, slightly taller than Sara, came into the room. 'Oh, Sara . . .' she began. And then Sara had another shock.

The girl was speaking Welsh. It was much too fast for Sara to understand anything, just like when she pressed the wrong button on the TV and got Welsh Channel 4 instead of English. Sara rubbed the ring, just in case the magic would let her escape.

As she rubbed the ring, something strange happened in her mind. She could still hear the Welsh words, but they started to make sense. The girl was telling her to stop hiding upstairs and come down, because somebody was coming—Sara didn't know who—and they would ask for *calennig*. This word made no sense to Sara, but she followed the girl anyway. At least she had *some* chance now of working out what was going on.

She hoped *calennig* didn't mean *ring*, or she really would be stuck.

She followed the girl downstairs and into the kitchen. It wasn't quite like Sara's own kitchen, more like the one she had seen at the Welsh Folk Museum, but not as big. The cooker was all black and there were tall tins of flour and stuff on a shelf, all white and blue. There were no brightly coloured cereal packets or fridge magnets. In fact there didn't even seem to be a fridge.

A woman in the kitchen, who seemed to be the other girl's mother, smiled at Sara. 'I thought you'd got lost,' she said, still in Welsh. 'I'd better give you something to keep you going. It's after eleven now, and those boys still haven't come.'

She gave her a thick slice of bread and butter. The bread wasn't bendy like normal bread and Sara kept dropping crumbs. She was surprisingly hungry. Maybe going back in time always made you hungry.

Sara realised that she had said '*Diolch yn fawr*' instead of 'Thank you very much'. Was the magic making her speak Welsh, as well as understand it? She wondered about saying a few more words, to see what happened, but she couldn't think what to say.

The only thing in her mind was the dragon ring bringing her back in time, but she decided not to talk about that. The woman might not believe her. After all, if someone went up to Sara's Mum and said they'd travelled back in time, whatever would Mum say?

She was just thinking this over when a loud knocking sound made them all jump. The girl took Sara's hand and ran with her out of the kitchen and towards the front door. She opened it to see a group of boys standing there grinning at them. One of them, Sara couldn't imagine why, was holding a large apple with little sticks pushed into it. As she stared at it, the boys began to sing:

Blwyddyn Newydd Dda i chi,
Ac i bawb sydd yn y tŷ . . .

Sara knew a few songs in Welsh, but not this one. She found she could understand the words, though:

Happy New Year to you,
And to everyone in the house.

Actually, she already knew the words *blwyddyn newydd dda*. She remembered having to write them on some Christmas cards they made in school. *Nadolig Llawen a Blwyddyn Newydd Dda.*

The woman had joined them by now, and stood there with them, smiling, as the boys sang another song. Then she reached into her apron pocket. 'Here's your *calennig*. One penny for each of you.'

The pennies didn't look at all like pennies. They were much bigger, and all new and shiny.

'Happy New Year to you as well, and make sure you say the same from me to your mother,' she added, as they turned to go.

'Do they sing ordinary carols as well?' asked Sara. (Yes, she was speaking Welsh, and they were words she didn't know. It felt weird.)

'Well, yes, before Christmas. But they only get new pennies for the New Year.' The woman sounded surprised. 'Didn't they come to your house last month?'

'No,' said Sara, truthfully.

'That's strange. Anyway, my dear, you must run off home now. Your Mam will be expecting you.'

Sara's mouth went dry. She didn't know what to say. This woman seemed to think she was the other girl's friend. What would she say if she knew where Sara had really come from?

'Are you all right?'

'Yes,' said Sara faintly. She stepped out onto the pavement.

'Goodbye, then. Happy New Year.' The woman shut the door.

Sara couldn't believe it. She found herself starting to cry quietly as she walked down the road. Whatever would happen to her now? She didn't know where or when the ring had taken her and she had no idea how to ask it to take her home. What would happen if she couldn't get back? What would she eat? Where would she sleep?

She wandered on. Nobody seemed to be around. At the bottom of the road she found nothing but fields, with stone walls around them. Sara sat on one of the larger stones that had fallen off the wall and dried her eyes. She must *think*. There must be some way to get back.

Just in case, she tried rubbing the ring and saying '*Dewch gyda'r ddraig*' again. Nothing happened. She took the ring off and said it.

Nothing.

Then she put the ring on, held up her hand, and tried a third time. (Third time lucky, Dad always said.)

Still nothing.

'*Please*!' she said. 'Please, dragon, or whoever you are.'

Nothing happened. Sara shivered, partly with cold, partly with fear. She had not the faintest idea what to do. She watched the smoke rising from the chimneys of some of the houses, where people were probably having their lunch. And her family, back home, were downstairs watching TV and didn't know she was stuck in another time and place. All because of a stupid dragon ring.

'It's not fair to bring me here and just leave me,' she wailed, out loud. 'If that stupid ring hadn't said *Come with the dragon* then I wouldn't have . . .'

She held her breath. The mist was starting.

A minute or two later the thick cloud around her had cleared. There was her own bedroom again, full of her own things. She was sitting on her bed, next to her toy pink hippo. It was all real. She was safe. She picked up the hippo and hugged it with relief.

'Sara?'

For a moment, Sara froze in panic, but this time it was Mum's voice. Mum came into the room.

'I thought you—what's wrong?' She stared at Sara and the hippo. 'Have you been crying?'

Sara shook her head.

Mum sighed. 'I don't know why you've got yourself in such a state over that carol-singing. It isn't worth worrying about. It's only that I don't want you wandering off on your own.'

'It's all right,' said Sara. 'I'm OK.' She followed Mum downstairs.

If only you knew, she thought.

Chapter 6

Sara found it all rather hard to believe the next day. Going back in time just didn't happen. It was like one of those stories where you couldn't really think how to end it so you wrote *And then she woke up and it was all a dream*, except Mrs Hughes had a nasty habit of saying 'Try to think of a *proper* ending, Sara.'

Perhaps it was a dream. Perhaps she had just fallen asleep on her bed when she went upstairs.

She kept thinking about it in school and was much quieter than usual. Louise didn't notice because she never bothered about anything like that, and Mrs Hughes didn't notice because she was worrying about the songs for the Christmas concert.

Sara didn't spend too long talking to Louise at the end of the day. As soon as she could, she escaped to her bedroom and took out the ring.

Was it really magic?

There was only one way to find out. She would have to say the Welsh words again and see what happened. She slipped the ring onto her finger.

Just in time she stopped herself from saying the words. She hadn't yet worked out how to get back to her own time again—she might get stuck in the past!

Sara shivered as she realised what she had

nearly done. She took the ring off again, just to make sure, and thought as hard as she could. What had she been doing just before the mist started again and she found herself back in her room?

She had been sitting on a stone at the end of a road. She hadn't done anything much, but she had said something. Something about how upset she was.

It would make sense if there were words you had to say to get home again, because you had to say *Dewch gyda'r ddraig* to go back in time. It couldn't be *Dewch gyda'r ddraig* both times, because she had already tried that.

Sara shut her eyes tight and tried to work it out.

She had said something like: 'It's not fair. If the stupid ring hadn't said *Come with the dragon* I wouldn't have come here at all.'

Maybe . . . maybe it was the words *Come with the dragon*. If you said it in Welsh you went back in time and if you said it in English you came home again. That just about made sense. It didn't quite make sense, of course, because she lived in Wales anyway and . . .

Sara sighed. It was very complicated.

The question was, did she have the nerve to try it out?

She decided to go ahead before she could change her mind. She put the ring onto her finger and said '*Dewch gyda'r ddraig*,' firmly.

The mist began straight away, almost as if it had been waiting for her. Sara stood there impatiently until it had cleared. She was surprised not to see the old room again; this time she was standing on a damp hillside, and it was raining slightly. Wisps of mist (the ordinary wet sort, not magic mist) floated past her, which was a bit confusing.

It was not a very exciting trip this time. But then she hadn't really meant to go anywhere; she just wanted to see if her idea worked. She looked down at her clothes. Old ones again, and quite soggy already. Maybe this was a time before anyone invented umbrellas.

Quickly she held up her hand with the ring on it and shouted 'Come with the dragon.'

The mist swept right over her and cleared, a little more slowly. It worked! She was home again!

Sara hurried into the bathroom to find a towel. Her own clothes were dry, but her hair was dripping wet. She didn't want Mum to notice her using the hair dryer.

Her hair was not very dry by the time she went downstairs. Mum gave her a funny look. 'Why is your hair wet? You only washed it last night, it can't possibly need washing again.'

Sara couldn't think of anything. She shrugged her shoulders. 'It just got wet. I'll go and dry it properly.' She raced back upstairs before Mum could say anything else.

She sang to herself above the noise of the hairdryer. The words to '*Blwyddyn Newydd Dda*' were still in her mind. Mrs Hughes would be dead impressed if Sara sang her a new Welsh song. However, she would want to know where Sara had learnt it.

If only people didn't ask so many questions . . .

A thought crossed Sara's mind suddenly. If she had been able to speak and understand Welsh in that other house, would she still know how? It had seemed so easy then, she felt sure it was possible. It would be brilliant if she could speak Welsh without having to learn it. She would be the best in the class, even better than Rhian.

Later that evening she decided to try it out. She flicked through the buttons on the TV, looking for Welsh Channel 4. She had just found it when Mum and Dad came in.

'Switch it over to number three, Sara,' said Dad.

'Oh, *Dad*!' Sara grumbled.

'Hurry up, love, there's something I want on in about thirty seconds.' He held out his hand for the remote control. Sara handed it over sulkily. 'I don't know what you're fussing about,' he added. 'You can't have been watching anything. This is the Welsh channel.' He pressed a button and the adverts started.

'I *was* watching it,' Sara muttered.

'Ssh!' said Mum.

Sara gave up. Anyway, it was more important for her to be able to *speak* Welsh brilliantly rather than following a television programme. She decided to try it out as soon as she could. Louise would be really jealous if Sara started getting team points for remembering all the words.

Chapter 7

The next morning Sara was about to ask Mrs Hughes if they had Welsh, but stopped. She had asked her exactly the same thing the day before, and Mrs Hughes didn't like her class 'going on about things', as she put it. Sara sighed. It was Friday. If she waited all weekend, the magic might wear off or something.

Her luck was in. Straight after assembly, Mrs Hughes said, 'Right, all of you, listen carefully. You all need to finish off your sentences from yesterday, and after that, if you get them all done, you can do a handwriting card. But you must get a move on, because I want to do Welsh for twenty minutes before play. We haven't done any this week.'

'Yesss!' said Sara happily, but not too loudly in case Mrs Hughes noticed.

Louise noticed, however. 'What's so exciting about handwriting?'

'I meant the Welsh,' said Sara.

'You're hopeless at Welsh!' said Louise. 'You get loads of words mixed up.'

'I do *not*.'

'You do.'

'Are you two going to get on with your work, or do I need to split you up?' Mrs Hughes interrupted coldly.

'Get on with our work,' Louise muttered. She made a face at Sara and went off to sharpen her pencil. Sara didn't care. She'd soon show Louise.

Sara only just managed to finish her English before Mrs Hughes told them all to pack away. She left her work tidily on her table and hurried over to the carpet, taking care to sit up straight and fold her arms so Mrs Hughes would notice how good she was being.

'Well done, Philip, Sara, Rhian and Leanne.' Mrs Hughes sat down. 'Hurry up, the rest of you. That's right. Now, we were learning about houses last week. Let's see if you can remember how to say "I live . . ." in Welsh.'

Sara's hand shot up.

'No, Sara, I meant all together. Say it with me: *Rydw i'n byw . . .*'

Sara realised that the one time she had a chance of remembering everything, Mrs Hughes was going to say all the words for them first. She listened to the Welsh and couldn't work out whether she really knew it, or whether she was just repeating it. It was very annoying.

After about ten minutes of going through saying their addresses and the types of house they lived in (which was dead easy because they were almost the same words, like bungalow which sounded the same but you just spelt it in a funny way), Mrs Hughes said, 'I think it's time we had a quiz. Let's have the blue team sitting on my right, the greens on my left and the reds in the middle.'

They all started to wriggle into the right places. 'Don't take too long,' Mrs Hughes warned, 'or you won't have time to win any points.'

Sara swopped places with Louise and sat in the middle. Louise, who was in the green team, moved closer to Rhian.

'I want to see how many of the words about food you remember from September,' Mrs Hughes began. 'And you must put your hands up, or you'll lose a point. Blue team first: what does *losin* mean?'

She pointed to Philip. 'Sweets,' he said. Sara wriggled. She knew that one.

'Well done. Red team, it's your turn. What is *teisen*?'

'Cake!' Sara called out.

Mrs Hughes gave her a hard stare. 'Sara Roberts, I warned everybody two minutes ago that if you didn't put your hand up you'd lose a point. I can't very well give your team minus one, but nobody is to shout out again. Green team's turn.'

Some of the red team groaned quietly. Mark poked Sara. She poked him back. He was about to poke her again, but saw Mrs Hughes looking at him and stopped. Sara was furious with herself. Her team stayed one point behind for the next few minutes and though she put her hand up every time, Mrs Hughes didn't ask her anything.

'Blue team: what's *carrot* in Welsh?'

Wesley put his hand up. '*Moron*,' he said, giggling.

'I know it's a silly word,' said Mrs Hughes as some of them joined in the giggles, 'but he is right. Red team, what's the word for *ice cream*?'

Sara stretched her hand up as far as it would go and saw Mrs Hughes nod towards her. Her mind went blank suddenly. She *had* to know this one. '*Pysgodyn*?' she said uncertainly.

'Remind me never to go shopping with you, Sara,' Mrs Hughes said kindly, 'because I can't imagine what you'd end up buying. *Pysgodyn* means *fish*.'

The whole class burst out laughing. Sara wanted to die, especially when Rhian said the correct answer, *hufen ia*, and Louise whispered, 'We're three points ahead of you now!'

Sara's face was burning. She put her hand up. 'Mrs Hughes, it's not fair.'

'I'm afraid I can't see why. You got the question wrong and Rhian got it right.'

'But Rhian used to go to a Welsh school. She knows lots more Welsh than we do.'

'I'm not going to argue with you, Sara,' said Mrs Hughes, 'but I've got two things to point out. One, Rhian has had two goes this morning, exactly the same as you. Two, I'm testing you all on words you learned this term, not words you've never heard before. If you had gone to a Welsh school I expect you'd have forgotten most of it by now.'

Sara looked at the carpet. Mrs Hughes was being horrible. Louise was horrible. She'd probably go and play with Rhian now instead of her. *Everyone* was horrible.

Why had she forgotten all the Welsh, when she could speak it yesterday? That was the trouble with magic. It always let you down at the wrong moment.

The bell for play soon brought the Welsh lesson to an end. Sara trailed down the corridor behind Louise, who was walking arm in arm with Rhian. Louise turned round. 'Stop following us,' she said.

'How else do you expect me to get to the playground?' retorted Sara.

Louise stopped walking. 'I don't care, but don't follow us. We're not your friends.'

'It wasn't my fault I couldn't do the Welsh!' Sara muttered.

'Who cares how many you got wrong? You're not in our team.' Louise glanced at Rhian and patted her arm kindly. 'We're not friends with you, Sara, 'cause you were horrible to Rhian and she was really upset. It's not her fault she went to a Welsh school.'

They hurried into the cloakroom to get their coats. Sara stared after them. She hadn't even thought about *Rhian* getting upset.

And now everyone seemed to hate her.

Chapter 8

Sara often went to the park with Louise on Saturday mornings, but the day started off cold and damp. Sara was secretly relieved. She didn't want to see Louise, and she didn't want Mum asking questions.

It might be more fun going back to the past again. That other girl had been nicer to her than Louise usually was. And now she knew how to come and go as she wished, there was nothing to worry about.

She wrote PRIVATE KEEP OUT on a piece of paper and left it outside her bedroom door, just in case someone came looking for her when she was in the past and thought she had been kidnapped or something. If Mum or Dad read it they'd think she was making Christmas cards or something like that.

She shut the door and fetched the jewellery box from the cupboard. Placing it carefully on the floor, she took out the ring and put it on. '*Dewch gyda'r ddraig*,' she said, and watched the mist thicken. Would she go back to the old house again this time?

But as she wriggled her feet she could feel rough stones beneath them, and a cold wind blowing. And then she heard shouting. It was almost like listening to her friends shouting in the playground.

The mist cleared.

It was a playground she was standing in. Children were running round looking just the same as they would in any playground, except that the girls' skirts were long and the boys wore shorts, and the colours of their clothes were dull. Sara examined her own clothes: a longish navy skirt, a pair of boots with a patch on the side—and then she had no more time to think. The bell was ringing and all the children were rushing over to the door at the end of the building, anxious to get inside out of the cold.

Sara hesitated. It was Saturday, after all (or, at least, it was Saturday at home). Did she really want another day in school?

Just then an older girl seized her hand. '*Come on*,' she said, in Welsh. 'Mr Jones will be cross if you stay out here.'

Sara obediently followed her. They stood silently at the end of the two lines of children. The man by the door stopped ringing the bell and nodded at the first pair, who started to walk in. Sara noticed them glance towards the wall and quickly smooth down their hair; when she entered the porch, she saw there was a round mirror hanging on the wall with *Am I Clean and Tidy*? painted above it. For once Sara found she did look fairly tidy.

She was still walking beside the other girl, but as they went into the classroom the girl whispered,

'You're on the left side, with the younger ones,' and gave her a little push in the right direction.

Sara found herself on an uncomfortable wooden bench in the front row. She realised, as she sat down, that the girl had just spoken to her in English. This was very odd. She had definitely said something in Welsh earlier, so it must be a Welsh school.

She sat up straight (it seemed like the sort of place where you had to) and watched Mr Jones. He had fair hair which stood out against his dark suit, and no smile. Sara suspected he did not smile very often. She realised Mrs Hughes wasn't too bad really.

'Sara Roberts.'

Sara jumped, then realised Mr Jones was calling the register. '*Yma*,' she said clearly. Mrs Hughes usually made them answer the register in Welsh, so she was used to it. It would be a good idea to keep on the right side of Mr Jones.

A gasp went round the room. There was a long and terrible pause.

'Well, Sara Roberts,' Mr Jones said quietly, but not kindly. 'What language were you speaking in just now?'

'Welsh, Mr Jones,' Sara answered, puzzled and a little frightened.

'You are *able* to speak English, then.' His voice was still dangerously quiet. 'Which is just as well. Because we do not speak Welsh in school.

School is for civilised children. Civilised children speak the Queen's English.'

Sara wasn't sure what 'civilised' meant. She didn't dare ask. Why was Mr Jones so cross about one little word of Welsh? Anyway, he seemed to have finished now, and he wasn't going to shout at her. He was picking up a board from a shelf with a rough loop of string hanging from the top.

'The usual punishment for you, Sara,' he said, beckoning to her. Sara's heart pounded. She stood up unsteadily and made her way to the front. Mr Jones hung the board around her neck. She could feel the string digging into her, scratching her every time she moved. She looked down at the board. WELSH NOT, it said.

'You know how to pass this on, and if not, it's the cane for you after lessons. That will teach you to STOP SPEAKING WELSH IN SCHOOL!' The sudden shout startled her. She felt the string rub her neck. She twisted her hands nervously and, to her horror, felt the ring slip to the floor.

The room was silent enough for Mr Jones to hear the ring clatter. He picked it up. 'And this bit of rubbish . . .' For a moment Sara thought he was going to throw it in the bin, but he saw her face and changed his mind. 'I shall let you take this after school, but if I see it again it will stay in my desk. Now sit down, and let me have no more trouble from you for the rest of the day.'

WELSH NOT

Sara just could not believe this was happening to her. She let the board rest awkwardly on her lap. The string was really starting to hurt. Why, why had she come back in time again? Last time had been fun, except for getting stuck out in the cold. This time was awful.

How was she to know children weren't supposed to speak Welsh in whatever year it was? And why not? Mrs Hughes was always pleased if they remembered to ask to go to the toilet or something like that in Welsh. Rhian spoke Welsh at home, but she was much better at English than Sara. What on earth could Mr Jones have against it?

They were all having to copy some words from the board now. Sara had to use a funny grey pencil-shaped stick which didn't make marks except on her slate. Year 6 had tried writing on slates for a Victorian project and they thought it was great, but it wasn't any fun when you had to write lots of words very tidily. And the slate kept squeaking and Mr Jones kept looking at her.

If only she could escape. But she didn't have the ring, and she wouldn't get it till the end of the day.

Sara suddenly remembered. Mr Jones hadn't just said she would have her ring back after school. He had said she would have the cane, unless she could pass the board on! And she hadn't a clue how she was supposed to do that.

Chapter 9

Playtime began at eleven. Sara's board felt heavy before she even reached the playground. She wanted to sit down, but realised she must find out from someone how to get rid of the board so that she wouldn't have the cane.

It was not easy. She didn't know anyone, and every time she went over to speak to someone they ran off to play with someone else. At first she thought she was imagining it, but after it had happened four or five times she decided that it was true; for some reason, nobody was talking to her. So she sat by the wall to rest her neck, until it was time to go in.

The second half of the morning dragged on even more. Lunchtime was worse than playtime. All the other children had brought something to eat in a brown paper parcel or a tin box; a pie if they were lucky, bread with cheese or jam if nothing else. Sara sat in her place by the wall and tried not to watch them talking and eating. She was desperately hungry, and there was a sore mark on her neck even when she lifted the string out of the way. And she still couldn't get rid of the board. She buried her face in her hands.

She felt someone tap her shoulder, and looked up to see a boy, a year or two older than her. He was looking hard at her tear-stained face. 'What's wrong? Did you forget your dinner?' he asked.

Sara nodded. She usually had school dinners, but they didn't seem to exist here.

The boy unwrapped a paper package. 'You may as well have a sandwich, then. Mam always puts in plenty. She thinks I'm working down the pit already and wanting a man's dinner.' He smiled at her. Sara gulped the sandwich down in huge mouthfuls, so hungry she hardly tasted it. It was only the one sandwich, but a good solid one.

'Is that better?' the boy asked.

'Yes,' said Sara, but then she remembered the board again and her face fell. 'I don't know how . . . what do I do to get rid of this board?'

The boy stared. 'Of course, you're new, aren't you? Haven't you been to school before?'

'Of course I have!'

'Didn't they have the Welsh Not in your old school?'

Sara shook her head. 'You're lucky,' he went on. 'If you still have it by the end of the day, you get the cane. The only way you can get rid of it is to hear someone else speaking Welsh and tell on them. Then they get the cane instead.'

'But nobody will even let me talk to them! Why won't they . . .'

'What do you think? They don't want the cane!' He saw the look on Sara's face. 'It isn't that bad. It hurts, of course, but you get used to it. And he probably won't hit you very hard as you're a girl. He may even let you off,' he added, doubtfully.

'I suppose he might,' said Sara, without any real hope. She gave the boy a small smile. 'Thanks for the sandwich, anyway.'

'That's all right.' Some other boys were waving to him. He ran off towards them.

I don't even know his name, Sara thought.

It was boring sitting by the wall, but anything was better than sitting in class with Mr Jones about to call you up to the front for the cane. All too soon the bell started to ring. Sara got slowly to her feet. Mr Jones himself was ringing the bell and everyone was hurrying into line.

Sara didn't hurry. The board made it awkward to walk. All the children's eyes were on her as she made her way to the back of the line. Her face was red and blotchy but she didn't care any more what she looked like.

'What's wrong, Sara?' asked a voice quietly but clearly as she joined the other children.

It was the boy who had given her the sandwich. And he hadn't spoken in English. He had said, *Beth sy'n bod*?

Sara stared at him with a mixture of hope and alarm. He had done it on purpose, she was sure, and now she wouldn't get the cane . . . but *he* would.

'Well, Owen Phillips, we have two forgetful children in school today.' Mr Jones's voice was cold. 'Step out of line, if you please.'

Owen stepped to the side. He avoided everyone's eyes.

Mr Jones lifted the board from Sara's neck. 'Let that be a lesson to you,' he told her sharply, before placing the string on Owen's neck.

The class walked in silently, though a few braver children nudged each other and pointed at Owen or Sara.

The end of that afternoon stayed in Sara's mind for ever. Weeks later she would wake up in the middle of the night with her heart thumping, hearing once more the swish of the cane on Owen's back, seeing his knuckles white where he

gripped the desk and the red marks under his shirt which he showed the other boys after school.

She was the last out of the building, the ring once more safely on her finger (she had wondered if Mr Jones was going to keep it). She saw Owen walking painfully along the road ahead of her, a group of friends round him. She started to run after them, but the other boys shouted at her and she turned back.

Sara held up the ring and said the magic words. She just hoped Owen realised how grateful she was to him. She would never have a chance to tell him so.

Chapter 10

She was back. Back in her own colourful bedroom. No more scary Mr Jones; he was gone forever.

I'm never going back in time again, Sara thought. She carefully put the ring back in her jewellery box (even if she wasn't going to use it, she didn't want to throw it out) and found half a bar of chocolate behind the box that she had forgotten. She broke off a few squares. All those hours with only a sandwich had made her hungry.

All those hours . . . Sara panicked, almost dropping the chocolate. What on earth would Mum and Dad think? Had they been in her room and found she wasn't there? Had they phoned the police?

'Mum!' Sara dashed out of her room and straight downstairs, almost falling over herself. 'Mum, I'm here!'

Mum came out of the kitchen. 'So I see. What's all the shouting about?'

'I . . .' Sara stopped. Why wasn't Mum a bit more glad to see her after all that time? 'I'm back. I'm all right.'

'Back from where?' Mum gave her a funny look. 'I think I'd better get you a clock for your room. You've only been half an hour making those cards, you know.'

Sara's mouth dropped open. She turned her head towards the wall. The clock said eleven o'clock.

'I thought it was lunchtime,' said Sara.

'It's nowhere near.' Mum wiped a smudge from the corner of Sara's mouth. 'And you can't be that hungry if you've been eating chocolate. Come and have some squash.'

Sara drank the squash in about five seconds. 'I haven't quite finished the cards,' she said.

'I should hope not!' said Mum. 'They'll look much better if you take a little more time over them. Anyway, you need something to keep you busy for a while. It's still pouring with rain.'

'OK.' Sara raced back upstairs. Probably magic always did funny things with time. I wish I knew more about magic, she thought. Then she remembered Mr Jones and the heavy board, and changed her mind. There was no point in knowing more about magic, because she wasn't ever going back in time again.

She found some thick cream-coloured paper in her cupboard that would do for cards. It might be a good idea to make some now, if that was what Mum thought she had been doing.

Card List, she wrote on the top piece of paper. It was a bit crumpled anyway so it wouldn't have made a very good card.

Mum and Dad

Nan and Grampy

James

Mrs H

She could never remember how to spell Hughes. She would have to copy it from the classroom door. Mrs Hughes definitely deserved a card. She was quite nice really.

Louise

Sara wondered if Louise would really want a home-made card. She might be happy with an ordinary bought one. Mum usually bought some small cards for Sara to give to her friends. It was only special people who got home-made ones.

Rhian

Rhian could have a special card. Sara felt sorry for upsetting her. She wondered if Rhian missed her old school. It must be fun to speak two different languages.

If all the teachers in Victorian times were like Mr Jones, lots of people must have given up speaking Welsh. And in the end nobody would have spoken it at all. It must have been really sad for the people who thought their language was going to die out for ever.

So when we learn Welsh in school, Sara thought, it's like bringing a language back to life. That was amazing. Like magic!

She only wished Owen could know about them all learning Welsh.

Chapter 11

'Are you all right?' Mum asked Sara the next morning, watching her picking at her cornflakes. 'You've got shadows under your eyes.'

Sara shrugged. 'I was having a bad dream,' she said, stirring the cornflakes round and round in the milk.

'What about?'

Sara shrugged again.

Mum sighed. 'Oh well, whatever it was, I expect you'll forget all about it soon.' She stood up and started piling dishes into the sink.

Sara ate another spoonful, then stopped again. 'I don't think I want these.'

'*Are* you all right?' Mum asked again.

'Yes, I'm just not hungry!' said Sara crossly. She pushed back her chair and hurried back upstairs. She was even more worried now. What if Mum was right and she forgot all about Mr Jones? If she used the ring again after all, and something worse happened?

She took the ring out of its box and held it in the palm of her hand. It looked ordinary, just pretty, if you didn't know its secret. In fact, if she hadn't cleaned it in the first place and written out the words, everything would have been all right.

So . . . what if she could get rid of the words? Would that stop the magic working?

She was just thinking about how to do that when Mum came in. Sara shoved the ring into her pocket, trying not to look guilty, but Mum wasn't really looking. 'You haven't been sick or anything?' she asked.

'No,' said Sara. 'I'm all right. I think I'll come and get a drink in a minute.'

'Well, you just have a quiet morning,' Mum said. 'Finish off those cards or something. Your dad's said he'll help me put up that shelf in the kitchen, so we won't be doing anything else.'

Sara wandered downstairs after Mum, the ring still in her pocket. She noticed that Dad had actually got as far as taking out a tool-box, which was really unusual. 'What's in this box, Dad? I've never seen it before,' she grinned.

Dad grinned back and stuck his tongue out at her. 'Shut up,' he said. 'If you want to be useful, you can tell me where my small screwdriver's got to.'

Sara fished around in the box. 'Is this it?'

'No, that's a file.'

'What's it for?'

'Filing things down, of course,' Dad said. 'Smoothing them off. Whatever.' He took the file from her and peered into the lower part of the box.

'Can I borrow it for ten minutes?' Sara asked.

Dad stopped peering at the box and stared at Sara instead. 'What on earth do you want a file for?'

Sara thought hard. 'To rub down a pencil box. An old wooden one. Then I could polish it or something.'

Dad went over to the corner cupboard. 'You don't want a file for that, you want sandpaper. Here you go.' He handed Sara a rough grey piece.

Sara hurried upstairs with the sandpaper and her drink before Mum thought of asking about the sandpaper. She always wanted more details about why you were doing anything.

She slipped the ring out of her pocket, tore off a small section of sandpaper and rubbed the inside of the ring hard. At first it seemed to be going wrong; the sandpaper made the surface brighter and the dark words stood out more clearly than ever. But slowly, as Sara rubbed and rubbed, the letters faded at the edge, until after about fifteen minutes you couldn't read them at all.

But had she actually got rid of the magic?

Sara knew she should say the words once more, just to test it. But she didn't dare. She put the ring back in the box instead.

At least it had to be a bit safer now.

Chapter 12

Sara started being so good in school the next Monday that everyone wondered why. Even Mrs Hughes noticed, which didn't usually happen. Mrs Hughes noticed people like Rhian being good because they always were, so she didn't have to think about it. And she noticed people like Mark being good, because they were always naughty. But if you were somewhere in between, like Sara and Louise, you could be good for ages and nobody actually said you were.

Sara was the first to sit up straight, the quietest child in the line, and even her writing was tidier. She was nice to Louise, and Louise was nice as well as she had forgotten about the argument. (They had so many they sometimes forgot whether they were friends at the moment or not).

Nobody asked Sara why she was being so good. This was just as well, as she didn't want to tell anyone about it. She wasn't actually trying to behave better; it was just that every time she was about to mess around, or talk when she was supposed to be quiet, she saw Mr Jones's stern face in her mind and felt the sore mark on the back of her neck.

She learnt all the words to *Silent Night* in Welsh.

She finished most of her work in time.

She played with other children as well as Louise. She let other children play with them if they hadn't got anyone else to play with. It had been horrible to sit in that cold playground with none of the others talking to her except Owen.

She soon had a whole long line of team points.

Mrs Hughes started giving her nice tidying jobs at the end of the day. Not things like picking up all the bits of paper off the floor, but fun jobs like finding the right colour top for all the felt tips and testing them to see if they worked. 'I'll give that job to someone sensible, like Sara,' Mrs Hughes said, more than once. Sara couldn't believe it the first time she heard it.

Mrs Hughes was in a much better mood anyway once the Christmas concert was over. She let them all bring games to school, and on the last day she came in wearing a Father Christmas hat and gave them chocolate coins as presents.

Over Christmas, Sara almost forgot about the dragon ring. She visited relatives, watched all the good films on TV, ate nuts and tangerines until she was fit to burst, and soon the old year was over.

On New Year's Day she remembered the boys who had come to the house to sing *Blwyddyn Newydd Dda*. She asked Dad if there were New Year carols, like Christmas carols, but he just said, 'I don't think so. I've never heard any.'

I have, thought Sara. But she decided not to tell him about them.

Sara started thinking once more about the ring, even though she couldn't use it any more. She reminded herself that she hadn't really enjoyed her adventures that much, and she never got to choose where she went. The ring, or the dragon, or whatever, seemed to make its own decisions. It always took her back in time, and always somewhere in Wales. If it was a Welsh dragon it probably wanted to stay in its own country.

It was the beginning of February before Sara started to wish she had left the words on the ring after all.

Chapter 13

In the first week of February, Mrs Hughes sat them all on the carpet at the end of the day to tell them about the Eisteddfod competitions.

'There are a lot of competitions this year, but we should have plenty of time for them all. Who remembers when we have the Eisteddfod?'

A few hands went up. Mrs Hughes pointed at Philip. 'Is it March the first?' he asked doubtfully.

'That's right. And we also call the day Saint . . .' Mrs Hughes paused for them to tell her the answer.

'Saint David's Day,' they chorused.

'Well done. Now, let me see. There are two craft competitions, but you can do those at home over half term, so I won't tell you now. We'll start learning a song for the singing competition tomorrow, and there's a recorder piece for those of you who play it.'

Sara couldn't play the recorder. She had started it when a lot of the others did, but she lost her recorder for about three weeks and when she found it again, all the others had learnt five more notes and she couldn't really keep up. She thought she might enter the singing, though.

Mrs Hughes was still explaining things. 'We can do the handwriting in the next few days, and the art competition at the end of next week.'

I bet we're going to draw daffodils, thought Sara.

'But the main one you need to think about now is the poetry competition. That's the one for the whole school, of course, so usually someone in the top class wins it, but there's still a certificate for the runner-up in each year.'

Leanne put her hand up. 'Is that the one where you go up on the stage and you have to wear a cloak?'

'That's right.' Mrs Hughes smiled at her. 'It's the bardic poem, so the winner is crowned as bard

of the year. It's a very ancient ceremony.' She looked at her watch. 'There's no time to tell you much more. I'll just tell you the title of the poem you have to write this year: it's "Past Times".'

They all looked at each other. It was a funny title. Louise put her hand up. 'Are we writing it in school?'

'Yes, you'll have some time next week. But I'm not going to go over the ideas in much detail. You really need to think this one out for yourselves, as it's a whole school competition.' She saw their worried looks. 'Oh, all right then, I'll give you a few ideas. You could write about how things were different in the past, especially in Cardiff, or somewhere in Wales. You could pretend you're travelling back in time, I suppose.'

The bell rang.

'We'll have to leave it for now. Let's see who's sitting up ready to go.'

Louise and Sara walked home together.

'I'm definitely going to enter the recorder competition,' said Louise. 'You can't do that one. You can do the singing, though.'

Sara nodded. She couldn't think of anything but the poem.

'And you can do the handwriting, except mine's better than yours. Don't you think the poem's difficult?'

Sara went pink. She didn't want to talk about that. 'There's lots of time to think of ideas,' she said. ‘Anyway, I’ve got to go now. Mum said not to hang around so much.’ (This wasn’t true.) She turned the corner and walked backwards along her road, waving to Louise, until she felt dizzy and had to turn round the right way.

All the way home, Sara thought about winning the competition. She *had* to be the biggest expert in the school on past times. Nobody else could have actually visited the past!

Chapter 14

It was Wednesday night and there was nothing much on TV. Sara decided to start on her poem. She found a notebook with quite a lot of space in it and sat on her bed, thinking. She wrote *Past Times* at the top of the page. Then she thought a bit longer.

Then she wandered downstairs again and into the lounge. Dad was reading the sports section in the paper. 'Dad,' said Sara.

'Mmm?' said Dad, not looking up.

'I've got to write this poem . . .'

Dad's head appeared from behind the paper. 'It's not much use asking me. Go and ask your mum. She was always good at writing in school.'

Sara trailed out of the door. She found Mum in the dining room, but Mum was on the phone and looked as if she was going to stay there for hours.

Sara went and sat on the stairs, because it was less comfortable and that might make her get on with writing more quickly. She found her page again.

Past Times

Last time

I went into past times

Well, at least it rhymed.

Last time

I went into past times

I had a nasty time

It was true, and it rhymed. But it sounded a bit silly.

A teacher called Mr Jones

Sara got stuck. What rhymed with Jones? Bones? Moans? Phones? No, phones weren't any good, they hadn't been invented then.

Mrs Hughes didn't actually say it had to rhyme. Maybe it didn't have to. She scribbled the words out and started again on a new page.

Past Times

I went back in time

With my magic dragon ring

No, that was no good. Louise might start asking questions about the ring and it was nothing to do with her. Sara wanted to keep it as her secret.

She couldn't imagine what Louise would say if she knew about the ring. She wouldn't believe her, of course. And Sara couldn't even prove it without going back in time again. So Louise would just think she was either a baby or a liar.

Sara stretched her arms. It was very uncomfortable sitting on the stairs and it wasn't helping her to write at all. She was beginning to get cross with herself.

She tore the page out and scrunched it up. Then, to her relief, she saw Mum had finished talking on the phone and was just coming out of the dining room.

'Mum?' said Sara. 'Can you help me?'

'What's wrong?'

'It's this poem. We've got to write a poem for the Eisteddfod. I don't know where to start.'

'It's supposed to be your poem, not mine,' Mum pointed out, but she took the notebook from Sara anyway and went back into the dining room. She sat at the table and read through the front page, silently. Sara could see her trying not to laugh. She realised she hadn't torn out the first poem. She stared at the table. The poem wasn't that funny.

'I'm sorry, I can't really write it for you,' said Mum. 'Does it have to be about past times? It's quite a difficult title.'

'I know,' said Sara. 'Can't you give me some ideas? Dad said you could. He said you were good at poems and stuff like that at school.'

Mum laughed. 'I used to be, but that was years ago! I won the poetry competition when I was eleven. The bardic competition.'

'Really?' said Sara. 'So you had Eisteddfods just like we have now?'

'That's right.'

Sara took a deep breath. 'I wish I could win the competition,' she said. 'It's difficult writing about the past, though. If . . . if I could go back in time or something, it would be easy.'

'Well, there's no use wishing that, because you can't,' said Mum. 'Anyway, it wouldn't really help. It isn't knowing what the past was like, it's knowing how to write about it. And that means thinking about the best words to use, saying them to see how they sound, and all that.'

'I made it sort of rhyme,' said Sara. 'Past and last and all that. But I got a bit stuck.'

'Poems don't have to rhyme, you know. It's much better to think through your ideas properly.'

'I know,' said Sara, a little impatiently. 'Mrs Hughes keeps telling us.'

'Hadn't you better think what you know about the past first?' said Mum.

'OK,' said Sara. She stood up. 'I'll think about it myself for a while.'

'I think that might be a good idea,' Mum said.

Chapter 15

Sara still couldn't decide what to write the next day. Why couldn't she think of any ideas?

She walked along the road to her house, still thinking it over.

Maybe the ring would still work, even when it hadn't got the words on it. If she went back just once more, maybe she would meet someone in the past who could help her. It was worth trying.

She found the ring still in the box. Carefully she put it on her finger. She wasn't going to be silly enough to drop it again. '*Dewch gyda'r ddraig*,' she murmured, and held her breath as she saw a small swirl of mist.

Then the mist disappeared again. Nothing happened.

'*Dewch gyda'r ddraig*,' she said, louder. Again, just a wisp of mist, then nothing. The magic really had gone!

In a way, it was a relief to know the ring couldn't do anything now. But Sara felt a bit disappointed as well . . . and what was she going to do about the poem, without anyone to help give her ideas? If only she could have seen Owen again! He might have told her something exciting to put in. She might have seen him a few years further on and he could have told her about working down the pit.

Suddenly she had an idea. Supposing she wrote down what Owen might have told her? It might sound just right. She shut her eyes and imagined him once more, then got out her notebook and began.

> Today I have to say goodbye
> To the slate pencils and rows of desks.
> Today I'm going to the pit.

She stopped and thought. 'Squeaky slates' would sound good. And he could have said goodbye to the playground as well. She was just looking for a rubber to change a few words, when she heard Mum calling. She opened her door and leant over the banisters. 'What?' she shouted.

'Auntie Cath's on the phone,' called Mum. 'She wants to say hello.'

'Can't you say hello to her for me?' Sara called back.

'Don't be silly! Come down and talk to her.'

Sara hurried downstairs. She liked Auntie Cath, but she wished she could have rung a bit later.

Auntie Cath mainly wanted to know what Sara wanted for her birthday, as Mum hadn't given her any ideas. Sara, for once, hadn't even thought about it. She promised to ring back later in the week to let her know.

Putting the phone down, she wandered into the kitchen to get a couple of biscuits. 'Don't spoil your tea,' Mum warned, watching Sara's hand creeping into the tin. Then she looked more closely. 'What's that?'

'What's what?'

'What's that on your finger?'

Sara felt her heart pounding. 'It's only a ring.'

'I can see that. What I want to know is where you got it from.'

Sara couldn't think of anything to say.

'Let's have a look at it,' said Mum, very firmly. Sara realised it was no use trying to say no. She took the ring off silently and handed it to Mum.

'Good heavens,' said Mum. She turned the ring round. 'A dragon . . . That's funny, the inside's all shiny, but the rest isn't.' She inspected the dragon

again. ‘Sara, this isn’t any old ring. It’s valuable. Where did you get it?’

Staying quiet wasn’t going to work. Whatever was she going to say? She couldn’t tell Mum she’d found it, Mum would make her take it to the police or something.

Sara had a brainwave. ‘Louise gave it to me. She said I could keep it.’ Mum couldn’t do anything about that.

But Sara was wrong.

‘Oh, Sara, I can’t believe you’ve done this again!’ Mum sounded really cross. ‘I don’t mind you swapping stickers and things, but you must not swap anything valuable.’

Sara felt like crying. Everything was going wrong.

‘Don’t you remember when you gave Louise your new book, and she wouldn’t give it back? I thought you’d learned your lesson that time.’

Sara hung her head.

‘Put your coat on. We’re going round to Louise’s house right now.’

‘But Mum!’ Sara began, horrified.

‘Hurry up. I don’t know what Louise’s mum is going to say.’

Sara trudged along the road behind Mum, trying desperately to think of a way to get the ring back. She couldn’t think what to do. She could only hope that Louise’s mum would say it wasn’t her ring. But then what? Down to the police station? Or would Mum keep the ring?

Mum rang the doorbell of Louise's house. Sara stood miserably behind her.

'Sorry to bother you,' said Mum, as the door opened. 'Sara's come home with a ring, and I think it belongs to Louise.'

'Probably,' said Louise's mum, standing back to let them in. 'I know what they're like for swapping things.'

'It's quite old,' Mum said, holding it out.

Louise's mum took the ring. 'Her gran gave her a whole lot of old jewellery for dressing up just before Christmas. That's probably where it came from.' She turned towards Louise, who was just coming into the room. 'Louise, did you give Sara this ring from your gran's jewellery? You're not to give any of it away, or I'll tell her to stop giving you all those things.'

Louise took the ring. 'Sorry, Mum,' she said. She slipped the ring onto her finger. Sara watched her in alarm.

'I've told Sara not to do it again,' said Mum.

'And I'll have a talk to Louise about it,' said Louise's mum. 'Thanks for bringing it back.'

Louise followed them into the hallway. Sara managed to stay just behind Mum. 'You can't take my ring,' she whispered to Louise in desperation. 'It's got a special secret. I've got to tell you . . .'

'I don't care about your stupid secret,' Louise whispered back. 'You lied to me about that ring, you said you hadn't got it, and it serves you right now you've really lost it. I'm keeping it now. And I'm not your friend.'

'Oh, come on, Sara, you'll have plenty of time to talk to Louise tomorrow,' said Mum. She took hold of Sara's hand and marched her down the path.

At least, Sara told herself, she'd had one last chance to make sure the ring didn't work. However horrible Louise could be, Sara wouldn't have liked her to risk getting stuck in the past for ever.

She was glad not to have told Louise the secret of the ring, after all. Some secrets were best kept to yourself. And it was always possible the poem about Owen would win the competition, if she tried really hard.

Now that *would* be something to make Louise think . . .